Spanky and His Blanky

by Marissa Jo Cerar and Esme Cerar Monreal

Copyright © 2024 Marissa Jo Cerar and Esme Cerar Monreal

All rights reserved. This book or parts thereof may not be reproduced in any form, stored in any retrieval system, or transmitted in any form by any means—electronic, mechanical, photocopy, recording, or otherwise—without prior written permission of the publisher, except as provided by United States of America copyright law. For permission requests, write to the publisher.

This is a work of fiction. Names, characters, business, events and incidents are the products of the author's imagination. Any resemblance to actual persons, living or dead, or actual events is purely coincidental.

ISBN: 978-1-960157-71-3 (Paperback)
ISBN: 978-1-960157-72-0 (Hardcover)

Spanky and His Blanky

By Marissa Jo Cerar and Esme Cerar Monreal

1. Fiction

FIRST EDITION

Illustrated by Hanna Semenova

Published by Bookfox Press

Printed in the United States of America

For Spanky

And Scooter

And Tabby

And Sammy

And Lulu

And Winter

...and Esme, who loves animals with the fullest heart.

Spanky and his puppy pals, Tabby, Sammy, Jake, and Scooter, are chasing tennis balls when Spanky hears Winter call out, "Who wants to play tug of war?!" Tug of war is Spanky's favorite game, a game he could play for hours, but when Spanky turns around and sees what Winter is carrying, he can't believe his eyes.

Winter has what appears to be a dingy piece of fabric in her mouth, but that's not just any fabric! Spanky rushes over to Winter and with a sad growl he says, "No!!!! That's my blanky!"

Confused, Winter drops Spanky's blanky from her mouth. It's just a blanket. Why is Spanky so upset? Jake snarls. He doesn't get it either. It's not Winter's fault. "It doesn't even look like a blanket, it looks like trash!" Jake and his puppy pal Sammy giggle, teasing Spanky. "Only babies need their blankies!"

Embarrassed, Spanky grips his blanky tight in his teeth. Tears form in his eyes as he looks around. None of his puppy pals have blankies. They're all laughing and playing without any worries. Why can't he be like them? Maybe he is a baby. Spanky walks away from his puppy pals. Maybe Jake was right. Maybe only babies need their blankies. Maybe it's time for Spanky to grow up.

To fit in with the other dogs, he digs a hole under his favorite dogwood tree, buries his blanky, and scurries back to the play yard, proudly telling his pals, "I don't need that silly blanky. Let's play!" And he plays all day, just like his puppy pals. Maybe he really has outgrown his blanky.

Spanky tosses and turns all night. He can't sleep. Without playtime to keep his mind busy, all he can think about is his blanky. Romeo, his wise Husky roommate, can't sleep either... because Spanky's whimpering is keeping him up. Concerned, Romeo asks if Spanky is okay.

Spanky wants to tell Romeo that he's not okay. He wants to tell him that he can't sleep without his blanky—and that he can't remember a night or even a nap where he slept without it—but he doesn't want Romeo to tease him, so instead he says, "Of course I'm okay. I'm not a baby!" He then turns away from Romeo and pretends to sleep.

The next morning, a very sleepy Spanky enters the play yard without his blanky, but he still can't stop thinking about it. Instead of playing with his puppy pals, he sits under the dogwood tree, where he buried his blanky. Romeo snuggles up to Spanky and says that it's time to stop pretending. "It's okay to not be okay." Spanky starts to cry. "Why can't I stop thinking about my blanky? Why can't I play freely like my puppy pals?"

Romeo knows that Spanky has had his blanky since the day he came to the shelter... maybe it reminds him of home? Spanky is quiet. Home? For as long as Spanky can remember, the shelter has been his home. Romeo reminds him that he had a home before the shelter... Romeo did too. All the puppy pals did. But why can't Spanky remember his home? Romeo isn't sure, but he can see that the blanky gives Spanky comfort. Maybe if he had it close to him, it would help Spanky remember.

With Romeo's help, Spanky digs up the blanket. It's covered in dirt, but he's so happy to have it back! While Romeo and the other puppy pals eat lunch, Spanky lies on the blanket under the dogwood tree and finally falls asleep.

As Spanky naps, the memories of his life before he lived in the shelter come rushing at him. He remembers the last time he saw his mother. She nudged his blanky towards him and then left to go search for food. Spanky was alone for what felt like weeks when a human finally arrived to rescue him. He was scared at first because his mother always said he wasn't allowed to talk to strangers, but Spanky would have to learn to trust this human and other humans if he wanted to find a safe place to call home.

Spanky wakes up from his nap and barks for Romeo. "I figured it out! I know why I can't stop thinking about my blanky! The blanky reminds me of my mother and my home—before the shelter became my home." Romeo stands and he tells Spanky that it's okay to hold on to his blanky for comfort. Spanky gets an idea. "Maybe if the other pups knew, they'd understand too..."

Romeo watches from across the play yard as Spanky courageously tells the story of his blanky. After hearing about Spanky's mother and his life before the shelter, his puppy pals apologize for teasing him. They can all understand what it's like to miss someone you love. They're all rescue dogs, hoping to find their forever homes. After his friends apologize, Spanky feels free again—free to play!

On adoption day, the shelter is filled with humans, tall and small, hoping to find a furry forever friend.

Spanky wakes up with his clean blanket wrapped around him. One of the shelter workers must have washed it while he slept. Grateful, he rubs his sleepy eyes and discovers a family approaching.

Spanky's tail wags when he sees what's in the Little Girl's arms... her very own blanky! It's love at first sight. She beams, "What's your name, doggy?" The Shelter Worker says that he came to the shelter as Spanky, but she can call him whatever she wants. The parents interrupt, "If he came with the name Spanky, then that's his name. When you adopt a person, you don't change their name, right, Essie?"

The Little Girl, Essie, smiles, understanding instantly, "Umm, yeah! It would have been super weird if you had changed my name—super duper weird!" Essie opens her arms to Spanky, "Well, Spanky, are you coming home with us? I can't wait to show you our room!"

But Spanky freezes. He won't leave his crate. Essie is confused. Doesn't Spanky like her? Her mother tells her that Spanky will need time to adjust—just like Essie needed time when she first joined their family from foster care. "Spanky had a home before the shelter. He had a family, and then he made a family here too. We will become his forever family, but he will never forget where he came from."

While the family talks, Spanky tells Romeo that he's afraid his friends will forget about him. Romeo assures Spanky that they could never forget a special pup like Spanky, so Spanky grabs his blanky with his mouth and asks, "Wanna play tug of war?"

Spanky's puppy pals are confused. Tug of war? With Spanky's precious blanky? Romeo smiles. He knows exactly what Spanky's doing. He takes one half of Spanky's blanky, biting down on it with his teeth. Spanky does the same with the other half, and both pups pull Spanky's blanky until it rips in half!

Spanky then emerges from his crate and into Essie's open arms. "Let's go home, Spanky!" With his tail wagging, Spanky leaves half of his blanky with Romeo, explaining, "So you'll have something to remember me by."

With half of his blanky in his mouth, Spanky wags his tail and walks into his future with his forever family... taking one last look back at his forever friends.

As Spanky leaves the shelter, he trots past a woman wearing a neck scarf. She is instantly drawn to Romeo. With a warm smile, she reaches into his crate and fashions half of Spanky's blanky into a bandana for him, gently tying it around his neck.

As Romeo gets to know his new human, families are formed throughout the shelter, but one thing is for sure: Spanky, Winter, Tabby, Sammy, Jake, Scooter, and Romeo will never forget each other. Their time together may have been temporary, but the memories they created will travel with them wherever they go... wherever they call home. And while they may leave some things behind, no one can take their memories from them.

Spanky has had many homes. And each home meant something different to him. To Spanky, home is not really a place. Home is where he feels safe, where he feels loved, and where he feels free to be his truest self. And now, Spanky's home is snuggling in bed with Essie... and their blankies.

THE END

Questions for Little Ones

- Do you have a special something that you can't bear to part with?

- Has anyone ever made you feel shy or ashamed because of your comfort item, like Spanky?

Parents and Professionals

As an adoptee who grew up in a blended family (in which foster care had a significant impact), I know firsthand how important it is for children to see themselves in their favorite stories. However, sometimes seeing an exact replica can be too much for a child to process—it may be too close to their reality. That's why I chose to explore the subject of adoption and foster care through pet rescue. Friends have asked why we named our sweet rescue pup Winter. When I explain that she came to us with that name, we are often asked why we didn't change it. We wanted to acknowledge that Winter had a life before us, even if she can't tell us about her experience. Keeping her name, the one thing familiar to her, could be comforting in times of uncertainty, especially in the first few days, weeks, and months in a new home. In my experience, the same can be said for children. Having a "piece of home," whether it's a name, a story, a stuffy, a favorite food, or a blanky, can give a child a sense of comfort and stability when everything else in their life feels out of their control. Of course, I don't mean to equate the human experience to that of a pet, but sometimes we learn the most about ourselves through the stories of others. Learning to walk in someone else's shoes—or in this case, someone else's paws—can open hearts and minds.

I hope Spanky's story makes the children in your care feel less alone, even if only for a few minutes, while escaping reality with Spanky.

— Marissa Jo

Printed in the USA
CPSIA information can be obtained
at www.ICGtesting.com
LVHW070957181024
793465LV00037B/180